DARK HUNTER

THE CRIMSON WELL

WITHDRAWN

First published 2015 by
A & C Black, an imprint of Bloomsbury Publishing Plc
50 Bedford Square, London, WC1B 3DP

www.bloomsbury.com

Bloomsbury is a registered trademark of Bloomsbury Publishing Plc

A CIP catalogue for this book is available from the British Library

ISBN: 978–1–4729–0822–3

Typeset by Newgen Knowledge Works (P) Ltd., Chennai, India
Printed and bound in Great Britain by
CPI Group (UK) Ltd, Croydon CR0 4YY

1 3 5 7 9 10 8 6 4 2

recommended by

www.catchup.org

Catch Up is a not-for-profit charity
which aims to address the problem of
underachievement that has its roots in
literacy and numeracy difficulties.

DARK HUNTER
THE CRIMSON WELL

BENJAMIN HULME-CROSS
ILLUSTRATED BY NELSON EVERGREEN

A & C BLACK
AN IMPRINT OF BLOOMSBURY
LONDON NEW DELHI NEW YORK SYDNEY

The Dark Hunter

Mr Daniel Blood is the Dark Hunter.
People call him to fight evil demons,
vampires and ghosts.

Edgar and Mary help Mr Blood
with his work.

The three hunters need to be strong and
clever to survive…

Contents

Chapter 1   A Midwinter Journey   7

Chapter 2   The Stone Circle   19

Chapter 3   A Stone Axe   35

Chapter 4   The Crimson Well   50

Chapter 1

A Midwinter Journey

Mr Blood, Mary and Edgar stood by the side of the road. The coachman was shaking his head and staring at the ground.

"What do you mean, you won't take us there?" Mr Blood shouted. "That's what we are paying you to do."

"Then keep your money," said the coachman. "The stone circle is no place for us tonight. It is midwinter."

Mary looked excited. Edgar felt nervous. They were going to an ancient circle of standing stones. Mr Blood had not said why.

"At least take us a little closer," said Mr Blood.

The coachman shook his head again.

"Not tonight. The past six years at midwinter there has been…" His voice trailed off.

"Witchcraft?" Mr Blood asked. The man nodded. "That is why we are here," said Mr Blood. "To stop the witchcraft."

"I dare not take you any closer," the coachman said.

"You must!" said Mr Blood. "We will not get there in time if we walk. Take us as far as you can along the road and drop us near to the stone circle. Then we will deal with the witchcraft that makes you so afraid."

The coachman stared at the ground.

"Come on, man!" Mr Blood shouted. "I have two children with me who are less afraid than you."

In the end, the coachman said he would take them closer to the stone circle.

They got into the coach. The coachman climbed up behind the horses and they set off along the road once more.

It took a few hours to get there. Edgar and Mary asked Mr Blood to tell them more about where they were going but he shook his head. "It is very dark magic," he said.

At last the coach stopped again. The
coachman opened the door and they
got out.

"Follow the road and you will see a
track leading uphill," said the coachman.
"Follow the track. When it starts going
downhill you will see the stones."

Without waiting for Mr Blood to pay him, the coachman jumped back on the coach. He cracked his whip and drove away. Mr Blood, Edgar and Mary were alone.

Chapter 2

The Stone Circle

They followed the track until they saw
the stone circle. The tall, dark stones
looked like a circle of giants. It was late
afternoon and the sky was black with
clouds.

As they came nearer they saw a smaller circle of wooden posts, inside the stone circle.

"What do you think is going to happen?" Mary asked.

"Witches have met here at midwinter for six years." Mr Blood said. "This is the seventh year and seven is a powerful number in bad magic."

"Yes, but what are the witches trying to do?" said Edgar.

"I fear that they will try to bring out Evil itself," replied Mr Blood. "If I am right, they will make a sacrifice."

They reached the stone circle. There were twisting patterns carved into the stones. Edgar and Mary stared up at them.

"These stones were placed here hundreds of years ago," said Mr Blood. "This should be a place to worship the light, not to call evil into the world."

They walked on towards the smaller circle of wooden posts. The carvings in the wood showed beasts with huge, savage fangs. Edgar looked at a carving of a monster which was half human, half snake.

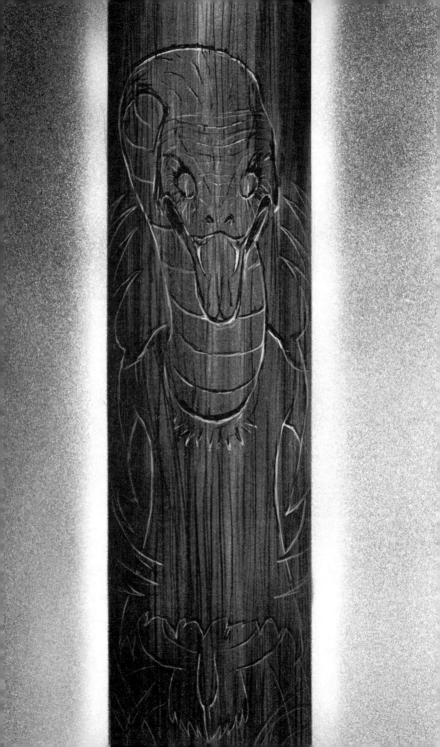

"Did the witches put these here?" asked Edgar.

"That's right," said Mr Blood. "They believe that all the evil in the world comes from a giant snake. They hope to call him from under the ground and set him loose. We *must* stop them.

Mr Blood breathed deeply. "If the witches raise the giant snake it will travel the world killing people," he said.

"Can nothing stop it?" asked Edgar.

Mr Blood shook his head.

"Once it is loose, the only way to stop the snake is to spill its blood in the place where it was called into the world."

"I'm thirsty!" said Mary. "Is this a well?" She went towards a small wall of stone in the centre of the circle.

"Careful!" Mr Blood snapped. "Don't drink from that. That is where they will make the sacrifice." Edgar drew back. Mary looked down into the well.

She gasped and jumped back.

"Why don't you both go and get some water we can drink?" Mr Blood said. "There's a stream a bit further down the valley. But make sure you're back before sunset. The witches will arrive soon after dark."

Edgar was happy to leave the stone circle for a while. He thought Mary might say that she wanted to stay. She liked it when things seemed scary. But she just nodded her head and ran off down the valley.

It was a few minutes before Edgar caught up with her.

"What's wrong?" he asked.

"The well," Mary whispered. "It was full of blood!"

Chapter 3

A Stone Axe

Edgar and Mary walked for a mile or so before they found the stream. Mary sat on a rock while Edgar filled their bottles. He was just about to step back from the water when he saw something.

"What's that?" Edgar said as he reached down into the stream and pulled out something heavy.

"It's a stone axe!" Mary cried. It had a smooth wooden handle and a dark green stone blade. On the stone they saw the twisting patterns they had seen carved back at the stone circle.

"Let's take it with us," said Edgar.
They began walking back up the valley. It
was beginning to get dark and they were
still a long way from the stone circle.

"Let's run," said Mary. "I don't want to
get caught on our own by those witches
after sunset!"

They began running but suddenly, Mary tripped. She fell sideways off the path and onto a large rock. She tried to get up but she couldn't.

"Are you alright?" Edgar asked. "Come on, we need to get back." It was getting darker.

"I don't think I can," Mary groaned. "My foot is stuck!"

Edgar looked down. Mary's ankle was trapped between two big stones. Edgar tried to push them but they would not budge.

"I'll go and get Mr Blood," said Edgar.

"No!" Mary cried. "Don't leave me here on my own. You heard what he said they were going to do tonight!"

"Well, we can't just stay here!" said Edgar.

"Don't leave me Edgar. I'm scared," said Mary. "You are never scared!" said Edgar. "I'll be quick. We're about ten minutes away from Mr Blood. That's enough time for me to be there and back before dark. It's the only thing we can do," he said.

Before Mary could argue, Edgar ran off along the path towards the stone circle.

As he got near, his heart nearly stopped. Mr Blood was there with a group of seven witches around him.

The witches moved in a circle, twisting rope around Mr Blood. *"They're tying him up!"* thought Edgar.

He hurried back to Mary and told her what he'd seen.

"We have to help him!" Mary said. "See if you can find something to push away one of the stones so I can get my foot free."

Edgar searched around for anything useful but could see only rocks.

"Edgar," Mary cried. "The axe! We can use the axe!"

Edgar picked up the stone axe. He pushed the wooden handle in between the two rocks next to Mary's foot. Then he pushed the top of the axe as hard as he could.

The rock moved just a little, but it was enough for Mary to squeeze her foot out.

"Can you walk?" Edgar asked.

Mary tested her ankle.

"It's sore but I'll be fine," she said. "Come on. We have to help Mr Blood."

Chapter 4

The Crimson Well

By the time Edgar and Mary reached
the stone circle, the sky above them was
dark. They hid behind one of the huge
standing stones and watched what was
going on.

The seven witches danced around the well, singing and chanting. Mr Blood was tied up and lying across the top of the well.

"What can we do?" Mary said softly. Edgar shook his head.

One of the witches stepped towards Mr Blood. She drew a knife across his cheek. Blood ran down his face and dripped into the well.

The witches stopped chanting. For a moment everything was still. Then the ground began to tremble. The witches howled with joy.

The standing stones and wooden posts shook. The head of a huge snake rose out of the mouth of the well.

Its jaws were wide open and as it rose, it swallowed Mr Blood whole.

Edgar and Mary both cried out in horror. They ran towards the huge snake.

One of the witches turned and saw them. She laughed. The snake kept rising out of the well. Its body was as thick as the trunk of an old oak tree. Its fangs were like an elephant's tusks.

The monster wrapped itself around the outside of the well. The head reared up, high above the standing stones.

The witches bowed before it.

Edgar reached the snake before Mary. He was still carrying the stone axe. He swung the axe at the snake's body.

The blade cut through scales and drew blood. The snake's hiss was like the sound of a huge waterfall.

The snake stared down angrily at Edgar and Mary, huge drops of venom dripping from its yellow fangs. The children trembled as they waited to die.

The snake froze for a moment, ready to strike, and then it began to sway. It made terrible choking noises. Edgar saw a bulge in the monster's neck.

Then the snake's skin split open and an arm came out of its neck, holding a knife. The snake hissed again and twisted around in pain. The knife cut through more of the snake's neck and the skin tore as Mr Blood pulled himself out of the snake.

Mr Blood gasped for air. He threw the bloody knife into the well and the ground began to tremble again. The witches howled.

The angry snake gave one final hiss and then thrust its head back into the well. The earth shook once more as the monster went back under the ground.

The witches ran away, and Mr Blood fell to the ground.

Mary rushed over to him and hugged him. "How... how?" she gasped.

"I knew I had to get some of the snake's blood into the well," said Mr Blood, "so I let the witches make me the sacrifice. I kept my knife hidden."

The moon came out. Mr Blood, Edgar and Mary were alone in the stone circle once more. Only the dripping blood on the well showed what had happened in that terrible place.